The Graves

J.P. Stevens

This is a work of fiction. Names, characters, places, and incidents either are the product of the author's imagination or are used fictitiously. Any resemblance to actual persons, living or dead, events, or locales is entirely coincidental.

Copyright © 2024 by J.P. Stevens

All rights reserved. No part of this book may be reproduced or used in any manner without written permission of the copyright owner except for the use of quotations in a book review. For more information, address:

Tanuci69@gmail.com

First paperback edition 2024

Anuci Press edition 2024

www.anuci-press.com

Cover Design by Mia Dalia

https://daliaverse.wixsite.com/author

ISBN 979-8-9905033-1-1 (paperback)

ISBN 979-8-9905033-2-8 (ebook)

PJ's Old Home Place

CHAPTER ONE
PJ

It all began in Columbia City, South Carolina, the year was 1971. PJ Parker was around 7 years of age. His life had been a dream so far. Stella, his mother, was PJ's world. His father Duke was the breadwinner of the family but there was one problem, it was Stella's infidelity. Usually, a few days of each week she'd entertain Colin in the family home while Duke was away, hard at work. Colin was the owner of a local funeral parlor, and Duke's employer. Most of the community knew of Stella's infidelities but not many knew of Colin.

Duke worked for a funeral parlor as a gravedigger. The relationship between the two men was amicable, they even admired each other's work ethics. It was a brotherly relationship, but at times they were at one another's throats. Duke had heard of Stella and Colin's relationship, but he paid it no mind, feeling that his employer would never betray him, nor would the wife he loved so dear.

One day Duke headed out for work, and upon his arrival Duke and Colin had a brief discussion concerning the business at hand. Afterward, Colin departed the cemetery, leaving Duke to begin his cemetery tasks. Nearly an hour into his duties Duke faced a major problem.

Someone had already been buried where he'd been digging. It was unfortunately a lost grave from decades ago. He was forced to halt operations until Colin returned to the grave site. After nearly another hour, Duke grew tired of waiting around for Colin to return. The digger decided he'd rather be home than sitting around in a graveyard. After the decision to return home, he was given a lift by his assistant Tim who had driven to the church in his personal vehicle.

Upon arrival at his home, there in his driveway, he witnessed Colin's long black Cadillac. On his lawn sat PJ playing with toys.

Hey boy! said Duke as he hastily made his way onto his front porch.

PJ stared at the house as his father entered the home. For a few moments everything remained silent, and then he heard the yelling of his father and the screams and pleading coming from his mother and Colin. There was a terrible one-sided fight between the two men. Although Colin tried defending himself, he was no match for the fit gravedigger.

After beating his employer to a bloody pulp, Duke commenced carving his body with a razor-sharp pocketknife which he always carried. Colin lay on the couple's bedroom floor, gasping for air as the blood bubbled from his throat lacerations. Yep, Colin had been mortally wounded. During the fight, Stella was able to somewhat clothe herself with a housecoat. After seeing her boyfriend take his last breaths she tried fleeing the residence, but it was no use.

Her agile husband was able to subdue her near the front door of the home. There he wrapped his huge, weathered hands around his unsuspecting wife's throat. As he looked into her eyes he continued to squeeze the life from her body. A few moments later her eyes were bloodshot and seemed to try and escape their eye sockets.

After a while, her eyes grew dark, as life left her body. As he released his grasp, he began to feel the sharp pain circulating throughout his two murderous hands. It wasn't until then that he noticed all of his blood as it made its way down toward his fingers. Simultaneously he began to feel the burning sensations throughout his facial and neck regions.

He'd been in such a blind rage he didn't realize before how Stella had diligently fought for her life. She'd broken each of her fingernails as she desperately tried freeing herself from his death grip. A movement from the corner of his eye broke the concentration he'd placed on his wounds which also caused him to flinch.

It was PJ. The poor kid was sobbing and nearing shock. He had witnessed everything, both murders. Duke was in such a rage that he'd developed tunnel vision during the fight. All his senses had now returned. Just as he reached out to embrace his only child he looked over to see the Sheriff along with several Sheriff's deputies, with guns drawn. Duke was then arrested without incident, while PJ was placed in foster care for nearly six years.

Although Duke had murdered his wife and employer, after spending the night in jail he paid a $500 bail and was released.

During those days, a respected and needed member of society, especially those who were law abiding, were often granted a pass for first time major offenses. Duke committed a crime of passion and most of the citizens of the city felt as though Stella was human garbage. During his trial, the broken-down digger was exonerated. Although he had been exonerated he was never able to regain custody of PJ, due to South Carolina state laws. Committing the murders was a tough blow mentally for Duke, but the citizens of the surrounding counties were very forgiving and supportive of the broken man; it wasn't long before a rival funeral home of Colin's hired Duke as their own digger.

It wouldn't be until PJ was 21 years old that he would reunite with his father. Of course, P.J wasn't in foster care until he reached 21 years of age. The reason he was away so long was due to his violent nature. At 17 years of age P.J engaged in a fistfight with his high school teacher. Although the teacher (Mr. Wright) outweighed him by at least sixty pounds, P.J beat Mr. Wright senseless.

After the fight Mr. Wright spent three weeks in the hospital. According to court records the fight occurred due to Mr. Wright constant degradation of the kid .

P.J was sentenced to five years in state prison for administering the beating to his teacher, however he was released early due to prison overcrowding.

Photo courtesy of Author E.N.Chanting

CHAPTER TWO

Fred Duncan was a prominent member of society. Not only was he the mayor of Columbia City, but he was also highly respected in the legal community. His life couldn't have been better until he decided to purchase a small run-down funeral home. Duncan's funeral home read a new sign located in front of the newly acquired buildings. The transitional period was now in play for this retired attorney and his new funeral home. Most of the small crew employed by the funeral home remained employed with the new owner. Everyone, that is except the gravedigger. The gravedigger was pretty old, no one knew exactly how old, but he remembered being a young adult when Hitler was taken down. The digger was spoiled and was given a free hand to do as he pleased by the prior owners. This was a part of what caused clientele issues for the business. But knowing that the new owner wouldn't tolerate his shenanigans; he decided to bow out gracefully and chose retirement.

Now that the digger had left the company, this left a mighty big hole to be filled by Fred. There weren't many with the expertise nor the equipment to dig graves in the area. Therefore, Fred began his campaign of getting the word out that he needed a new digger.

HEY YOU! Are you skilled as a gravedigger? Read newspaper ads and billboards. Still, weeks later there would be no takers for the gravediggers' job. But then Fred heard about a guy known as PJ. PJ was the son of a long-gone burial vault dealer and grave digger.

PJ had seen the billboards flyers etc. They were plastered all around the city, but he paid them no mind. He'd once worked with his father in what PJ used to call Dead Folks Business. But after finding out his father was working overtime demeaning him to anyone and everyone who would listen; PJ walked out on his father and the business. That was the day he vowed never to break open the earth for burial again. A mere five years later his father met with his untimely demise. It wasn't a big deal for PJ when his father passed. The old man had caused his kids plenty of mental anguish. They all were sacred because of the antics of their father. Although they did overcome the madness placed on them by their father, a void always remained.

Figuring that the PJ would give in, since his dad was no longer among the living. The brand-new funeral director decided to pay him an unannounced visit late that evening just in case he had been away earlier in the day. This was a big mistake, PJ wasn't unemployed. He would take small jobs which didn't have any paper trails. The ex-gravedigger had no other choice but to live this way. Back in the early 2000's he was injured and wasn't able to remain gainfully employed again due to the injuries he'd suffered. The former gravedigger wasn't really a good person, he seems to have no morals. PJ also had a hand involved in many illegal activities. One of those illegal activities, he was in the middle of when Fred pulled into his driveway. Seeing Fred's SUV pull in sporting extremely dark tinted windows caused everyone to flee. Everyone except PJ.

PJ was in the middle of a large drug deal as Fred arrived. Arriving unannounced really didn't sit well with the outlaws. Fred switched off his vehicle and stepped out onto PJ's sand covered driveway. Just as Fred would look up, he would be face to face with the barrel of a sawed-off shotgun.

What the fuck do you want, cop? Fred nearly died on the spot. I'm...I'm not a cop, my name, my name is Fred Duncan. I just...I recently purchased the Walker Funeral Home. Added the nervous director

After hearing the man plead for his life, PJ chewed the poor guy out and ordered him to get back into his vehicle and leave. Even though Fred had nearly been killed, and cursed to no end, he still left his business card and asked PJ to give him a call at his earliest convenience. PJ took the card and stared down the SUV as it hurried down the sandy dirt road.

Alright...it wasn't the law, it was Fred Duncan trying to give me a job, yelled out PJ. Slowly emerged were the two men who had fled earlier. There was a twenty-pound marijuana deal going on which Fred stumbled upon and nearly ruined.

Fred made his way back into the city and vowed to never visit anyone unannounced as long as he lived. Although he nearly gave up the ghost, he still prayed PJ would give him a call. After sipping on nearly half a pint of vodka to calm himself, Fred took dinner and prepared himself for bed. Disappointed that PJ never called, he decided to get some rest and resume his search for a gravedigger the next morning.

It seemed that as soon as his head hit the pillows he was fast asleep. Over in the wee hours of the morning, Fred's phone rang out. Being deep in his sleep, the caller had to place his call twice.

Hello? Stated Fred. "Yeah, wake up Bud," replied the caller. "It's PJ, wake up old man." "Oh, PJ it's three a.m. Can't this wait til morning?" Asked Fred. "Well hell it is morning," replied PJ. "You said at my earliest convenience, and this is my earliest convenience but since you can't wake yourself up, let's forget it." Stated PJ. Realizing what was at stake Fred pulled himself together and began to talk business with PJ. After much begging and pleading the two men agreed to meet at the funeral parlor around lunchtime to wrap up the deal. And sign on the dotted line

After the call, Fred was so excited that he couldn't get back to sleep. It seemed that finally, he'd scored. Finally, he'd have a digger for the company. Hopefully, he could start accepting bodies. His mind began to run amuck. It was nearly 4:30 at this point. Instead of waiting around in bed till 5 o'clock, he decided to get up and start his day.

CHAPTER THREE
MOBI
PHOTO COURTESY OF COLIN HILL

Throughout the morning, he inquired about the past of his would-be employee. As it turned out PJ became a globetrotter after leaving his father's company. This was strange being that he never made much money working with his dad. The rumor was that his trips abroad were furnished by organized crime figures. He was often accused and arrested by law enforcement but never indicted. For years it seemed that anywhere PJ turned up, death also followed. He'd often be arrested but released the very same day. The locals often referred to the ex-gravedigger as Mr. Untouchable. The attorneys who posted his bail or freed him were usually from L.A., New York, Chicago, etc. Most citizens were deathly afraid of PJ, being that his name was synonymous with death.

Once while vacationing in Croatia, he was detained for the disappearance of his traveling companions. But it wasn't long before he would be released for lack of evidence. Less than six months after his departure from Croatia, his companions were discovered in a watery grave by local fishermen. It soon became apparent that PJ was nothing more than a paid assassin.

Once, law enforcement located an eyewitness in the murder of a prominent citizen. The accused was none other than PJ himself. PJ was released on one million dollar bail, but days before the trial was set to begin the prosecution's

witness all but disappeared never to be seen again. Therefore, the murder charges against PJ were dismissed.

Those were all the stories Fred heard throughout the morning. Though it seemed that within the last year or so things had calmed down concerning PJ. All PJ's travels had come to an end. He hadn't left the States lately, he mostly stayed close to the home and the property he owned. Somehow PJ had obtained a nice home along with several vehicles; not to mention all types of equipment that could be used in building ponds, small roads and even digging graves. Although all the wild stories made Fred nervous he was adamant that PJ would be his gravedigger. He'd sunk a ton of money into acquiring the funeral home. So, he wasn't about to let wild tales about PJ cause him not to start recouping his losses. Things were finally looking up for the newly acquired burial company. It was about time for his meeting with PJ. He decided beforehand to not mention any of the escapades he'd heard his new digger may or may not have been involved in. At that very moment while staring into deep space. He heard the entrance door to the funeral parlor open and bang shut. It was PJ he was an entire twenty minutes early for the rendezvous with Fred. The meeting lasted less than three minutes. PJ walked into Frank's office and handed over a sheet of notebook paper with the prices he planned to charge for any labor concerning opening and closing a normal grave. Fred looked over the paperwork and agreed. In less than ninety seconds the talk of what was expected was over, which ended the meeting. It wasn't clear to Fred who was the subordinate in the matter. Needless to say, everything was all too clear to PJ. The following evening PJ was seen around town being entertained by several strangers. Something was amiss these guys were all white middle-aged gentlemen. They'd arrived by limousine and wore expensive jewelry such as Rolex watches and 24-karat gold pinky rings. Was it the mafia or record producers? Who knows, only time will tell.

Fred was finally able to begin renovations to the old rundown funeral parlor. Also, he'd begun to boast on spinning just tens of thousands to beautify the building. He'd also chosen to gloat concerning the acquisition of PJ. All of this was understandable. The forty-year-old outlaw was very knowledgeable concerning graves and the cemeteries of most churches. PJ decided to purchase several molds from old business acquaintances. This meant PJ could now manufacture and install his own burial vaults for Duncan's funeral parlor. After hiring a crew for his business PJ began to stockpile burial vaults. Fred would tell his would-be clients that PJ even ordered several 80-pound bags of a substance which would be added to the cement to strengthen his vaults by an additional 30%. It was a lot of work the mid-aged PJ had taken on for himself. But the outlaw digger passed all of the manual labor onto his crew, the only work PJ was involved in was using his small track hoe to dig the graves. Also, he took it upon himself to add the substance used to strengthen the vault himself. Strange? Nope he took on this task due to the fact that he also added bits and pieces of human bone to the potion. It was a way to also dispose of the skeletons of his prior victims. According to PJ, the mixture had to be just right. If shovel or jackhammer work was needed, those tasks were immediately passed on to his crew members.

After nearly six months in the funeral business, the duo of Fred and PJ became a household name. Their work was superior to any other funeral parlor within the state. Even though PJ's crew was very thorough, professional, and dependable, still one thing worried Fred. That was the sound that could be heard as the burial vault settled onto the floor of the grave. The sounds seemed to be that something was being cracked or broken. Fred's inquiry of the crackling was meant with laughter from PJ.

"You never know what may be embedded in the earth," replied PJ. "Sometimes we run into old graves which means old caskets. State laws require that we're required to place the old caskets back in the bottom of the grave," stated PJ.

"What about the bones," asked Fred.

"The Graves I'm speaking of are lost graves; most are upwards of one hundred years old. Then there are tree roots, hollow rocks, underground, etc. You have to realize the weight of a vault is around 15,000 pounds or better. That amount of weight would crush nearly anything it encounters underneath the earth," added PJ.

"Humm! I never thought about all that," replied Fred.

Hearing this settled the director's nervous system. It also gave him an explanation if anyone inquired about the noises underneath the burial vault and its permanent residence.

That's a load off my mind PJ. It makes all the sense in the world, added Fred.

Business was constant, many came to Duncan's from all over the state. The renovations were done, and the funeral home looked fantastic. The building looked nothing like its old self. Two new hearses and two additional family cars were also added. With all of the deaths, PJ was forced into hiring another crew and purchased another track hoe.

Then there was PJ! Every month he'd head out into the surrounding major cities. At times he'd travel much farther, traveling as far as 1800 to 2000 miles to reach his destination. He'd never stayed away long, usually overnight, but sometimes he remained in the cities for a few days. Once PJ hired a guy (known as Mobi), who seemed to be a drifter. No one knew anything about this Mobi or why he chose to visit Columbia City. Inadvertently PJ accidentally bumps into him at a local burger joint, causing him to spill his drink. After purchasing Mobi another drink the two men engaged in small talk as they walked towards PJ's Pickup which towed his small track hoe. Seeing that the piece of equipment was secured to its trailer by precarious means; Mobi offered his help and secured the track hoe expeditiously. Immediately PJ offered Mobi a job which he graciously accepted.

For months Mobi worked his way through the ranks of PJ's crew. As it turned out PJ was a knowledgeable and dependable hand. He'd often assist his boss in late afternoons delivering the vault to its grave for the funeral services the following day. It was a strange way of doing things but often after the vault was installed over the grave PJ would dismiss his assistants, which meant driving him home. Afterward, PJ would return to the cemetery in his car just before dusk. This also made Fred curious about why he would often wait until the cover of darkness to finish securing the vault in its grave. This particular time Fred would go on a reconnaissance mission concerning PJ and The Graves.. He desperately wanted to know why PJ always returned near dark. Unbeknownst to PJ, Fred owned the buildings and properties surrounding the church's cemetery. In one of those abandoned buildings, Fred found himself in a spot where he had a complete visual of his employee. Doing so would soon give Fred the shock of his life.

After feeling certain that no one was around. PJ opened the trunk of his car and dragged out a man who was still bound and bloody. Presumably, the man was no longer among the living. Fred used his binoculars to be sure the person was deceased; indeed he was. Afterward, Fred was positive the man had been killed. PJ wasted no time stuffing the deceased into the grave underneath the vault. Once the body was laid out so as to not obstruct the vault's downward passage.

PJ hastily lowers the vault midway inside the grave and then places the artificial turf in their respective places. Therefore, if anyone chose to snoop around no one would have a visual on the body underneath the burial vault.

My God mumbled Fred. How long has this been going on? So, he only took the job to hide his murdered victims! He added. He felt sick to the point where he vomited. Fred was also perspiring profusely, and he became very weak. After slowly making his way to his vehicle, he drove himself to a nearby hospital.

Everyone tried telling me, were the only words Fred would allow himself to muster. After the nurses checked Fred's vital signs he was rushed through the emergency room to receive immediate treatment. Seeing the shocking site at the cemetery may have indirectly caused Fred to suffer his first-ever heart attack. Soon the word would flood the streets concerning the

health conditions of Mr. Duncan.

Although Fred was sick and hospitalized he had people in place to keep the ball rolling. It wouldn't be long before PJ gave his boss a call while working with his crew. Fred seemed to be in good spirits, but he seemed distant, as if something was bothering him.

"PJ, we really need to sit down and have a long talk over the next few days," Said Fred.

"Oh yeah, about what boss? You wanna put me in the will?" Joked PJ. "Hell, no you Jackass!. You're doing things while under my employment that are not only illegal but also morally wrong." Added Fred. "You know exactly what I mean Mr. Double Burial," said Fred then ended the call. PJ immediately called his employer again.

After the 7th ring, Fred answered the call only to say, 'You're done you killer', then hung up and powered off his phone. After powering on his phone his phone instantly began to ring again.. He felt it wouldn't be wise to turn off his phone for the night due to his business situation. Although the night PJ would call every hour on the hour. The next morning PJ arrived at the hospital to pay his employer a visit. He arrives at the nurses' station only to find out that Fred had been released just 10 minutes prior.

"Damnit," cried out PJ as he hurried out of the hospital. Determined to catch up with Fred before he visited law enforcement. But law enforcement was the furthest thing from Fred's mind. Upon his hospital release, Fred anxiously drove to his funeral home and deposited himself behind his desk. It felt great to be back in his office. Soon after, his digger PJ entered the office with a grin.

"Well, the dead have arisen," remarked PJ. It was evident that PJ didn't understand the magnitude of what he'd gotten himself into. During the serious discussion the two men had embarked upon, PJ's wisecracks caused Fred to several times threaten to call in law enforcement. However, the persuasive nature of the digger causes Fred not to follow through with his threats. PJ ended the meeting with a threat.

"Look, old man, understand me and understand me well." Stated PJ. "There are people that I work for, people you surely wouldn't wanna cross. Ever heard of the Conovess Family or Terry Conovess. If you have any notion about telling anybody about what's been going on in those graveyards, you too WILL find yourself being planted under a vault... alive! Capiche? Don't cross me, Fred. I'm warning you!" At a loss for words, Fred could only nod in agreement, PJ gave a disparaging look as he exited Fred's office and headed home.

Scared out of his wits, Fred remained in his office keeping a bead eye on the sidewalk leading to the funeral home's entrance. Still shaken from his prior meeting with his employee, he decided to give PJ a call to assure him that his secrets were safe with him and that they would never speak of his misdeeds ever again. Hearing this pleased PJ.

"Glad that you came to your senses, boss. This way I won't have to inform my employers about our little talk," said PJ. "As long as you keep me safe I'll keep you safe, that's understood, right boss?" Added PJ.

"Understood!" Replied Fred. It seemed that now since Fred had uncovered the digger's little secret, he'd become bolder with his crimes. PJ lacked morals, better yet it seemed as if he lacked remorse or possessed a conscience.

Photo courtesy of PJ Parker

CHAPTER FOUR
FREDDY'S BACK

Since Fred was now back at the helm of his funeral parlor, the business returned to normal. A few days after Fred's release from the hospital his childhood friend passed away.. Of course, his loved ones chose Duncan to handle the funeral services. The homegoing services went off without a hitch. That is until the coffin was sealed into the vault and PJ began the task of lowering the burial vault. But after lowering the vault 2 feet it wedged on the side of the grave and refused to go any further. Apparently, PJ somehow didn't dig the grave as wide as he should have. Therefore, PJ awarded Mobi the task of going underneath the vault to widen the grave. With shovel in hand, Mobi shimmied into the grave and completed the task within a matter of a few minutes. But just as Mobi began to emerge from the grave both cables snapped into. There was an ear-curdling scream from Mobi as the vault slammed onto the grave's floor. As the fifteen thousand pound vault gave way it tore Mobi's body into. The tortured man's upper body lay paralyzed atop the vault's lid. He lay on his back while his intestines oozed their way over the remainder of the vault's lid. It was a gruesome sight. The blood escaping his body pulsated with every beat of his heart. The smell of blood and human waste filled the air. The loved ones attending the service were inconsolable seeing what had just happened to Mobi. Some who were in attendance ran from the scene. Others showed no emotion due to shock. There were those who were injured after they tried to flee but instead collided with hundreds of pounds of granite monuments. The injured Mobi quickly bled out and died. moments later. The entire area was flooded with first responders and of course local news crews. It was unbelievable. Everyone was sad and filled with emotions. Everyone except PJ. PJ stared down at the half of a man with one eyebrow raised. He never spoke until EMS pronounced Mobi deceased.

"Damn, I've never seen a som bitch die so fast," blurted out PJ.

You're a terrible, inconsiderate human being, you don't even deserve to be called a human being. Screamed a female EMS technician as she shook her finger at PJ. She continued giving PJ what for, as her eyes began filling with tears. Before she could finish her lecture she stormed off to regain her composure in the rear of an ambulance.

After the death of Mobi, of course, a formal investigation was launched. During the recovery of Mobi's lower extremities from underneath the vault, investigators discovered that PJ used very old cables to lower the vault. The cables were rusty inside out.

Not only frayed but also filled with rust inside. Never had PJ used faulty equipment before. No one could understand why PJ would do such a thing. It didn't make sense until Fred met with Mobi's loved ones in Chicago. As it turned out Mobi witnessed a murder committed by one of the ruthless crime syndicates in his hometown. Although Mobi was adamant about not testifying against the killer, he still feared for his life. Therefore, instead of being killed by the syndicate to ensure his silence concerning the murder.; Mobi decided to flee the state, he'd planned on moving to one of the southern states and starting a new life away from the syndicate. Once he fled Chicago, a price was placed on his head by the criminal enterprise in question.

It was then that Fred realized that PJ killed Mobi. It was all intentional, him digging the grave too small, and using faulty cables to lower the vault along with some of the really outlandish things PJ spoke of when referring to Mobi immediately following his death. It was such a waste of a young man's life. Not only did Mobi's death nearly ruin Duncan and the funeral parlor. But it basically put a bullseye on the grave diggers back.

Unbeknownst to PJ, Mobi's loved ones visited police detectives and shared with them the information they'd shared with Fred earlier. Within a matter of weeks, PJ would be arrested and charged with manslaughter in the death of his deceased employee. Not only was he jailed, but his other bosses were not at all pleased with the way he deposed Mobi. Therefore no one came to pay his bail this time. Therefore, he was forced to bail himself out of Saluda City's county jail. Having to pay his own bail made him realize that maybe he'd gone a bit too far this time. The feeling that he may have been left to fight his own battles not only angered PJ, but it also caused him to experience a feeling he never knew much about. That feeling was a sense of fear.

After the incident at Duncan's last funeral procession, his business suffered drastically. For months no one would choose Duncan's for their loved ones' homegoing services. After a while, Fred wouldn't even bother with opening the parlor every day. He just decided that he would attach a note to the parlor door that included his cell number in case he was needed. It had been eight months since the incident in the cemetery still everyone avoided Duncan's funeral home. All of that time PJ never dug a single grave. Therefore, he was forced into giving his crews their walking papers. PJ single-handedly forced two small businesses to close their doors. He was no longer his old chipper self. Not even the area's other desperate outlaws would further their criminal enterprises with the likes of PJ, they all seemed to feel as though PJ was a chronic disease. Whenever he walked into a room the whispering, finger-pointing, and staring began. The entire citizenship of Columbia City held him solely responsible for the death of Mobi. Several weeks later PJ sold his properties to move into a small mobile home two counties over. For the first time in his life, since his mother died he felt completely alone. On the day of his final departure from the home he once owned and loved, his dog Bingo refused to get in his owner's pickup as usual for the fifty-mile road trip. The black bully mix just continued to bark while trotting in wide circles around the killer

"Bingo you crazed dog, what in hell's wrong with you boy?" asked PJ. "Have you been bitten by a raccoon or something?" He asked the dog, as Bingo continued with his shenanigans. "I'm sick of this," said PJ as he hopped into his truck and slammed his door. The dog, noticing the PJ had hopped inside the pickup stopped mid-cycle and sat as he looked on at his owner.

"Well, are you coming or not?" Said PJ asking him again and opened his truck's door hoping Bingo was done with his nonsense. But as soon as he opened his truck door, the dog again resumed his barking at PJ while trotting in wide circles. This really angered PJ even further. PJ then started the engine and cursed the bully mix to no end.

You stupid mutt, I hope a pack of coyotes eat you for lunch. Yelled PJ. That's why you don't even know who your daddy is, you som bitch, and I hope ya get the mange and die, added PJ, as he continued his tirade. It was a sad display, but Bingo seemed to care less. As the demented PJ pulled out of the driveway and headed south, Bingo trotted out of the driveway and headed in the other direction. It was sad, deserving, and a bit comical. Even man's best friend had washed his paws with PJ. But he continued on while staring into his rearview mirror, watching Bingo continue his trot down the gravel road without a care. With hurt feelings, the ex-gravedigger continued on his way.

CHAPTER FIVE
NEW FRIEND TO THE FAMILY

Photo courtesy of Sage Marchant

PJ was now alone and an outcast, he felt as if he'd been betrayed by everyone he'd ever known. As he drove, all types of things crossed his mind. The disgraced ex-digger wanted to end the life of everyone who he felt betrayed him, even those he'd taken orders from to kill. It was ironic, just as he thought of his organized crime bosses his cell phone rang. It was one of his bosses.

PJ where are you asked by the person on the other end of the call? I'm here at your house, but it looks like you've picked up and moved on. I came here to introduce you to a new friend of the family. Where are you, kid? Asked his Terry

A new friend of the family and showing up unannounced, not to mention leaving him in jail to rot. All those things weren't adding up to PJ. He'd been in the business long enough to know that the family had decided to end their relationship with him. Ending their relationship meant the family had placed a price on his head. Undoubtedly the new family member was a new assassin or enforcer. This new guy was supposed to without a doubt kill the ex-gravedigger and take his place as enforcer. It was apparent that the family wasn't pleased with the way he disposed of Mobi not to mention being arrested for the killing. The family members were afraid that PJ would spill the proverbial beans for a lighter sentence. Therefore, he had to be silenced which meant killing him.

. Without saying a word PJ ended the call with his now ex-boss. Soma bitches after all I've done for those clowns now they wanna off me, thought PJ. Now he knew that heading to his new home was now out of the question. His old bosses were well connected and within the hour he knew that someone would arrive at his mobile home to try and take his life. He also felt that the phone call was sort of a heads-up. The caller really liked PJ and probably didn't want to see him killed. He was trying to give PJ a fighting chance. With that being said, he knew that if the family could locate him to terminate his employment, he would be in a world of trouble. The family knew of two locations where he'd hidden bodies. If he didn't move quickly, he was sure that those two bits of information would find their way to law enforcement. He knew that he had to move the bodies, but he had to do so under the cover of darkness. Also, the bodies were buried in a quarry owned by the family.

PJ knew of a place not far from the quarry where he could hide his pickup until nightfall. Afterward, he could put his plan into motion which involved liberating the bodies. Once darkness filled the skies. He retrieved a shovel from the bed of his truck and slowly and cautiously made his way toward the shallow makeshift graves. Normally the hike to the grave from his hideout would have taken around ten minutes. But the fact that he wanted to remain among the living caused the hike from his hideout to take nearly forty-five minutes. Once PJ reached the grave he was ecstatic. He hurriedly plowed his shovel into the earth, while attentively checking his surroundings. After shoveling much further than he should have it became evident that the bodies were no longer where he'd buried them. They'd moved bodies that had been buried, and they were probably moved long ago by the family. The reason being was so the family would always have control over PJ. Realizing that the bodies were no longer there nearly drove the killer into a frenzy. The missing bodies caused PJ tons of mental anguish. In his mind, the missing bodies were the last straw. He felt as if removing the bodies was more than betrayal; it was disrespectful. In PJ's little world, he felt that bodies were a part of him and that he owned the corpses.

Now that he felt as if he'd been violated, he wanted war with the family. Although there was no way he could win a war or even a small battle against the family, he began mental plans while hiking back to the hideout. Upon his arrival at his hideout, he was greeted with high-beam headlights which were coming from Terry's limousine. Not only one new member of the family but two new members greeted him outside the limo. Finally, a headshot was delivered by one of the enforcers which nearly covered the two men with blood splatter. PJ's limp bloody motionless body falls face-first to the blood soaked him. The two men were much larger than PJ, both were white, well over six feet tall, muscular, bearded and both carried aluminum baseball bats. As the three men surrounded the family's ex-enforcer, he felt like a caged animal. As Terry explained the reason he had to be disposed of, his eye darted around the men as he looked for an escape.

"PJ, the family feels as if you are now a liability. Your methods are reckless and places to much unwanted attention on the Conovess Family."

After giving his short and sweet speech the crime boss returned to the comfort of his limo. PJ knew he was in trouble, just as he drew back a fist, an aluminum bat with unspeakable force crashed into PJ's ribcage sending him crashing into the earth. Favoring his probably broken ribs, PJ was allowed to regain his footing.

"Are you ok?" asked one of the assailants as he chuckled. But before PJ could answer again the cold metal again collided with the side of the man's skull causing blood to spew from his ear and temple region like hot molten lava fleeing a volcano. Also, the smell of raw sewage filled the air, due to PJ losing his bowels. The sound of the bats colliding with PJ's body sounded like the cracking of a Louisville slugger as the bat collided with a baseball during a NBL game.

Get on with it! Yelled a voice from inside the limo. Hearing this caused the two would-be killers to commence the human beating. Again, the bat crashed into the side of his skull which caused his teeth and fragments of his gum to make their exit from the dazed and bloody PJ. As his body somersaulted it was again meant with more metal than met with the bridge of his nose. The magnitude of the was so dramatic that it caused both his eardrums to explode as PJ let out a mighty scream. One of the assailants raised his bat high over his head and struck the unfortunate PJ with so much force that the crackling of his skull could be heard ricocheting throughout the limousine. He had been killed by those he'd killed so many others for. The killers looked at one another, each exhibiting their own sinister grins, each spat on the dead man and rushed over to the awaiting limousine

CHAPTER SIX
THE SEARCH

Photo courtesy: Brandie She Travels For Lunch

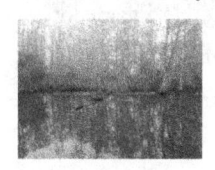

PJ slowly looked around as he used his hand to feel about his face and upper torso. It was all simply a dream or better yet a nightmare. while waiting for darkness he'd made himself comfortable inside the cab of his pickup and fell asleep. Still shaken by his nightmare, PJ retrieved his handgun from the pickup's glove box and cautiously exited the vehicle. It was pitch black that night and PJ could barely see his hand reached out in front of him. He hoped and prayed that the crime family were nowhere in the immediate area nor waiting to kill him. With gun in hand, he jogged all the way to the area where he'd buried the two corpses.

.After a few minutes, PJ finally reached the area where he'd buried the two corpses nearly a year ago. To his surprise the small gully where the two men's bodies resided was no longer a gully anymore, but a swamp. The entire area was unrecognizable. After wandering aimlessly, PJ finally realized and accepted that the bodies were lost; he had no clue as to where he'd planted the men before the erosion of the gully. Totally disappointed and some were heartbroken. The dilemma he faced could not be rectified. There was nothing to do but make his way back to his pickup and plot his next move. He desperately hoped that the crime family hadn't moved the bodies as they did in his dream.

"This is crazy," he said to himself. "How in the world can a gully become a full-blown swamp I just can't wrap my mind around this. God! I may be headed to prison, I'm willing to bet that those low lives had something to do with that swamp being where it is." After making his way back to his truck PJ reluctantly started his engine. Afterward, he drove out of the area. Unsure what to do next, PJ drove around the countryside pondering on what and where to go. He'd made lots of money working for Duncan's funeral home but what good would that do him. After touring the countryside, in total darkness it dawned on him, hitting him like a ton of bricks there was no choice but to leave the country, leave the United States and head overseas. This was the only way he could remain safe, but he had to find a place that did not honor the US extradition policies

Within a couple of days PJ had made his way through the Columbia City area and was now aboard a charter plane heading to Pakistan. Still intact with this life he did something he hadn't done since on this Earth. He thanked God for sparing his life. Unbeknownst to the Conovess family, (who searched the surrounding counties' diligently for the elusive killer) PJ was headed to freedom aboard. Having made prior arrangements with an old acquaintance, he now had a new place to call home. But little did he know his old acquaintance was also involved in organized crime. Within a few months, PJ was back to his old shenanigans, which was murder for hire. He was again his old chipper self. His ex-boss who ran the crime family was placed in the back of his mind. Within 6 months PJ had already murdered or disposed of three people. This guy was not a bad person, he was a terrible person. PJ was also a demented spirit. It seemed as though PJ had developed a reprobate mind. Even though the killer knew right from wrong, He'd done wrong for so long until wrongdoing was the only way his mind worked. All he knew was killing and being a conniving being. But after a year abroad his luck seemed to fade. The killer was spotted by a retired FBI agent. The agent was vacationing in the country with his family and happened upon PJ in a local bar. The retired agent just knew that the killer had no idea of his identity; therefore, he nonchalantly made his way through the bar to get a better visual of the killer in question. After passing PJ's table on several occasions, he was 100% certain that PJ was the fugitive sought by U.S law enforcement agencies. Those agencies had placed a large reward on PJ if he were to be apprehended. Although he'd been positively identified, there was still a major problem, the country where PJ now resided didn't respect the United States extradition policies. Therefore, it was up to the federal government to somewhat liberate PJ from his newfound freedom. Doing so would be next to impossible. It would require federal agents to basically kidnap the wanted killer and smuggle him back into the United States or at least to international waters. While the United States were busy figuring out a plan to kidnap and smuggle the wanted fugitive back onto U.S soil; PJ was busy setting up a reconnaissance mission. He was once again about to kill for the hire. The employer had high hopes of obtaining a large insurance policy from the death of his wife. This was morally wrong not to mention illegal, the task would net PJ upwards of $100,000. But this job wasn't as easy as the ones before. This time was a lovely, caring, middle-aged mother. Although PJ had reservations about taking the life of someone who was a loyal upstanding member of society, his greed and selfishness wouldn't allow him not to murder the unsuspecting victim. PJ thought about the woman for days wondering if he should allow himself to eliminate the only thing that was between himself and tens of thousands of dollars. After wrestling with what he figured was his conscience, his mind was finally made up

She's nothing to me. I don't know her from Adam, she could really be an evil person for all I know. He said to himself. Money couldn't be the only reason why her husband wanted her dead, he thought to himself. Although most people would have inquired further on what other reasons he wanted his wife out of the picture, there was another reason why the husband of the woman wanted her killed. The employer had committed several heinous crimes against his wife's family, he knew that there was only a matter of time before his wife sought help from law enforcement. This guy was just as bad a person as PJ. He knew that she would soon turn to law enforcement for their help. If so, he would undoubtedly face execution, a lynch mob or be killed in jail by others. His wife's family were also employed by law enforcement agencies. But this bit of information remained hidden from the unsuspected PJ. Within 24 hours PJ had again taken the life of another innocent victim. Although her husband had an airtight alibi he was detained, questioned, and arrested by local law enforcement. Although his incarceration was something most men couldn't endure; he remained tight-lipped about what he knew concerning his wife's departure; it was a sad, sorry occasion. Not only did PJ murder an innocent mother of three, he also disfigured her facial features to the point that her funeral services were a closed casket homegoing service. Her family members vowed revenge for the killing. This of course made PJ very nervous. He knew that if the murdered woman's husband cooperated with law enforcement he himself would be either jailed or killed in an inhumane manner. But the killer remained free for an additional 2 months before he was cornered by law enforcement. The husband had finally given in and named PJ as his accomplice in the murder of his wife. Not only was he arrested, but he was also brutally beaten beforehand. For several weeks PJ remained in a comatose state, News spread that a United States citizen had been jailed for the murder of a beloved citizen.

The news of PJ's arrest slowly reached law enforcement in the United States. Now that he was in police custody, there wasn't an urgency to liberate the killer from the uncooperative country abroad. PJ eventually regained consciousness, afterwards, he pondered on his life and the dilemma he faced in re-obtaining his freedom, which seems second to none. He knew there wasn't any way he would find freedom unless he left the jail in a pine box. Also, PJ had no clue that five of his murdered victims' relatives were employed by the city's police agency or the city's jail. The killer had no clue of how much trouble he'd gotten himself into me. Once released from the hospital PJ was again escorted back into the city's jail

Photo courtesy of Ruthanne Jagge

CHAPTER SEVEN
LAW- ENFORCEMENT

After regaining consciousness, it would be less than a week before PJ was turned over to unknown vigilantes who bound the killer and ushered him away from the jail. Under the cover of darkness, the killer was hidden in the trunk of a small compact vehicle, a vehicle that was once manufactured in the country of Yugoslavia. Once PJ reached his destination he was taken from the vehicle's trunk and ushered into what was undoubtedly a makeshift holding cell or better yet a cage made from angle iron. Just across the hall from the cage that housed PJ were 17 surgical instruments, knives made of surgical steel. Seeing those instruments was nothing more than psychological torture. All throughout the day PJ had a clear visual of the surgical instruments. Those instruments could very well end his useless life. This didn't help much, not at all, meaning that his mental state was in question; but seeing and wondering about the surgical instruments didn't help his mental status. Each time he heard footsteps leading up to his cage his heart sank, wondering was it time for him to be butchered by the knives that patiently hung across from of his cage

The conditions of his unofficial jail were deplorable; he was fed every two days, usually once during those days. On occasions he would receive two meals in a day. Needless to say, he was a shell of his old self. There was no way for him to bathe himself, a hole through the unforgiving concrete floor was his only means of relieving himself. Also, there was no running water, just the sweat of his cage that he would be forced to catch daily in case he chose to wash his hands after relieving himself. The jailers did not supply the fugitive with toilet paper... It was a terrible situation. Finally, late one night, better yet in the wee hours of the morning PJ was greeted by several visitors, he was beaten near unconsciousness, placed in handcuffs, and removed from his cage. Weak, battered and bloody the killer wasn't in any shape to fight or better yet defend himself from the men. It was a short walk that seemed to lead downwards. PJ soon realized that he was now in the basement of the building. He was laid out and scraped onto a medical table which was bolted to the concrete floor. A man dressed in blue stubs wearing a white laboratory coat appeared. He didn't say anything for a long while, he just stood there next to PJ smiling and glaring down at the subdued fugitive. After several moments the man spoke.

This photo is courtesy of Cornelius S.

CHAPTER EIGHT
DOCTOR DENNIS

"Hello, Mr. PJ," he said, while smiling, "My name is Doctor Dennis. I will be providing your surgical needs this evening."

The doctor was once very respected and well-to-do in the medical profession. He even was once a part of the medical team that cared for the needs of the president and first lady. Along the way something happened, no one is sure of what that may have been.

Years ago, while playing with his son Lucas, the five year old (from the window of his treehouse) sent a claw hammer crashing into the cranium of his dad Scott. That incident caused Scott a hospital stay, rehabilitation and of course there was some brain damage.

Then there was the golf cart accident where a party of drunk golfers T-boned Scott and his brother Chad as they drove their cart to the next hole. The impact sent Scott careening into the asphalt, while his head bounced off the unforgiving pavement.

Lastly, Scott Dennis was involved in a single car accident. In this crash Scott hadn't left work long, where he'd just completed a thirty-seven hour shift. En route home the weary doctor was to succumb to sleep. The doctor happened to crash through a guard rail which caused his body to be ejected through the windshield and somerset down an embankment.

All of these incidents Scott was involved in over the course of nine months. Also, over the course of two years after his last accident everyone could see a definite change in the doctor. He'd evidently quit the presidential medical team after accepting a position with the Vonbe crime family. In the beginning he was only in charge of seeing after the mob boss and his family, but eventually he became one half of the Vonbe crime family's torture team. Therefore, we have the evil Doctor Dennis.

PJ could hear laughter explode from the darkness on his left. "I understand that you've been admiring my surgical tools from afar since you've been detained here." The doctor then reached by his side grabbing a slanted cart and wheeled the cart next to the bound man. "Here Mr. PJ now you can easily get an up close and personal look at the tools of my trade." PJ's eyes seemed to swell as more uncontrollable laughter erupted.

"I'm terribly sorry for the delay Mr. PJ but I have been vacationing with my family in the United States and Canada."

"Have no fear, all will be fine, I will resume my holiday in the great United States once your medical procedures have been completed."

"Therefore, your look of concern is completely unwarranted. But there's one terrible bit of news that I must inform you of."

"My colleague passed away a few days ago without restocking the anesthetic agent.

What a selfish person, don't you think?"

"But, it will be fine, have no fear. I assure you that the anesthetic agent will not be necessary here." Added the doctor.

From my understanding, Mrs. Warren endured her procedure without painkillers.

As Dr Dennis rambled on PJ, wondered who Mrs. Warren was.

Then it dawned on him, Mrs. Warren was the woman he'd murdered not long ago. For the first time in his life, he felt remorse; also, it was the first time he'd ever heard of her referred to as Mrs. Warren. Where was this feeling of remorse coming from. Undoubtedly he always had a soft spot for women due to seeing his mother being murdered

His heart was heavy as he began to shed tears, not because of the murder victim but because of the pain and agony he was about to be forced into enduring. It was then that it dawned on him. He'd never ever harmed women and he had remorse for Mrs. Warren because of the fact that he'd seen his mother's life taken at the hands of a man, that man was his father.

Make yourself as comfortable as possible.

The doctor stated to PJ that he had to step away momentarily to make a phone call or two, and of course wash up for the procedures.

I'll just leave you to your thoughts, said the doctor.

As he stepped away, PJ could hear the chatter of the men who had conjugated to his left in the shadows. They were placing bets on how long PJ would live after Dr Dennis administered his surgical techniques upon him.

Then it happened. Out of the corner of his eye, he glimpsed them, a uniformed policeman along with a female officer from the jail he was once housed in. He remembered hearing from the so-called trustee Billy, who was a local petty criminal, and delivered meals to his cage, that Mrs. Warren's relatives were employed by the city's law enforcement agency. Right then he knew he knew that his goose was cooked. Not even law enforcement would rescue him from the torture he was destined to receive at the hand of Dr Dennis. The doctor reappeared drying his hands and forearms with what appeared to be a clean white hand towel.

"So how are we getting along Mr. PJ are you comfortable? Is there anything I can get for you before we begin," asked Dr Dennis. Needless to say, PJ never gave a reply. "Are you sure?" asked the doctor. "Okay then how about we get the ball rolling, this shouldn't take more than three or four hours with my coffee breaks and cigarette time included. If you remember, time is of the essence. I have a family to rejoin in the United States." With that being said the doctor removed a pair of scissors and began to cut away PJ's clothing as the detained fugitive began to wiggle around in hopes of freeing himself. Several of the policemen stepped out of the shadows and removed what was once PJ's clothing from underneath his body. There he laid exposed for the world to see...he was now stark naked!

As PJ's body laid on the cold steel table, his mind began to roam. He thought about all the people he'd hurt in his years as a hired killer. Not only those he'd killed but also those family members he'd hurt in taking the life of their loved ones. Never had he thought about all the people that he hurt in his murder-for-hire shenanigans. As he lay looking into the bright glaring lights overhead, he realized that his life was nothing more than a waste. PJ wished he'd never been born. He blamed his father for the hell which he was about to endure. But for some reason his mind was shaken, shaken like never before

He then realized that his father was not responsible for the mistakes he made, for the lives he'd taken. Those choices were his and his alone. After a few moments he realized that the doctor and the police officers were all at his side glaring into his eyes wondering what was going on in his mind. Never had they witnessed anyone there who appeared to be in a state of shock. After regaining PJ's attention, the doctor replaced the scissors and reached for one of one of his surgical knives. Dr Dennis applied a firm grip on PJ's right earlobe, next the doctor slowly placed the small knife against PJ's ear and slowly but cautiously began the task of removing PJs ear. Once the ear was removed Dr Dennis placed the ear on PJ's forehead and then positioned his body in

a way to comfortably relieve PJs of his other ear. As the killer's ears were being removed from his body, PJ trembled, not only from fear but also from pain. It was amazing due to the fact that the removal of his ears didn't spew blood but slowly and constantly oozed big globs of his blood. The pain was So intense that the killer made both hands into fist which exposed every vein in his hands, and bit against his teeth so hard that the enamel nearly shattered. But the ruthless killer Mr. PJ never cried out once from the pain.

Although he never cried out once, he prayed to get his hands around the neck of the doctor who placed his body in the hell he was currently in. If I could get just one hand around this broken English s.o.b. I could break his neck in five seconds. He quickly began to hate Scott Dennis and wanted nothing more than to cause him a slow and painful death

"This is by far the toughest one we've ever had here." Stated the quack Dr Scott Dennis. Next Dr Dennis begins admiring PJ's biceps and forearms "Okay, Mister PJ, now we will by-pass the remainder of the skull area and concentrate on the upper limbs. Would that be okay Mr. PJ? Do you have any objections?" asked the doctor. Again,

PJ never ushered a single word, but seemed to be in a trance as he stared a hole in the bright lights position overhead. "This is going to agitate you a bit more, this area here where the bicep meets the forearm we'll explore this region, okay Mr. PJ?" stated the doctor. Once again the doctor secured another surgical instrument but this time the knife was a bit larger than before. Once he obtained a sure grip on his surgical knife he seemed to heavily slice deeply into the area opposite the elbow. He commenced to slice deeper into the man's arm, until it was evident that he'd hit an obstruction, that obstruction was nothing more than PJ's bone.

This man undoubtedly was once and could still possibly have been a true doctor. Most would think cutting into someone's arms by those means would cause a person to quickly bleed out. But the doctor was very knowledgeable. He somehow maneuvered the surgical knife in a way that would bypass any vital veins and or arteries. The doctor wasted no time in again positioning himself as to begin to butcher PJs left arm as he butchered his right. But this time he seemed to have made a critical error. The doctor had sliced into a vital artery which caused the condemned killer's blood to squirt nonstop. Scott immediately began taking steps to stop the spewing of the blood of PJ. He seemed awfully worried that PJ would bleed out before he finished his butchery. Worried? It was likely so, he had strict orders to administer a slow torture to the killer. If PJ bled out before finishing his skilled knifing he undoubtedly would be next bound to the cold steel table. Luckily it took only a matter of moments for Dr Dennis to fix the blood spewing he'd caused.

PJ was now in so much pain it had to be unbearable, he now had his eyes closed both fish clutched and shaking or trembling uncontrollably. The only thing that helped with the pain was him daydreaming of administering the same mental and physical abuse to Scott Dennis.

The doctor then removed a large syringe and needle which he stabbed into the buttocks of PJ and administered a healthy dose of a clear liquid into the man as he seemed to lose consciousness.

Hours later PJ was awakened by someone placing a liquid-soaked cloth over his nose. PJ ears or where his ears once were had been bandaged. His ears had been disposed of as he slept. The incisions made by the doctor earlier were no longer open wounds Dr Dennis had sewn the wounds together. What a hell of a patch job, PJ slowly began to resemble the Frankenstein monster. Although PJ had awakened and was still in pain, the pains were no longer excruciating pains but somewhat bearable. The doctor informed PJ that it was time for his coffee and cigarette breaks again. After his break, the doctor again rammed the needle into PJ's body, again rendering him unconscious.

This time PJ wouldn't be awakened by the doctor. But soon he was awakened by pain from the incisions. During the time he was unconscious the evil butcher and his crew of corrupt police officers had unbound PJ and repositioned him onto his stomach before again bounding him to the steel table. The female officer, noticing that PJ had awakened, could be heard informing the doctor that his patient was again awake. It was evident that the doctor was waiting for PJ to awaken while he waited in another room. After PJ heard a door open and close in the shadows, he again heard the annoying condescending doctor's voice.

"Well, we've awakened, so let's get this thing wrapped up okay Mr. PJ?" Still there was no response from the wounded, near death serial killer. "Now we will focus on this area here behind the kneecaps," he said as he slapped on the man's leg. "Then once that's taken care of we'll focus here, just behind the ankles," he said as he again patted PJ on one of his ankles. "This won't take long at all. Then you'll be returned to the comfort of your room, and I can rejoin my family in the great US of A," said the doctor. The imitation Sawbones began to slice into the rear of PJ's legs but this time he didn't cut nearly as far into the killer's legs. One leg then the other, the doctor told him as he sliced into the man's body.

But this time the pain was so intense that PJ passed out from the cold surgical steel. Not realizing that PJ was again unconscious the blabbermouth doctor carried on with his medical stories.

"You do realize that this is what happens when you have a knee injury. Sometimes this is torn, and it needs to be fixed," he said as he sliced into the ligaments behind PJ's knee. He chopped into right leg then the other, or maybe he butchered one leg then the other. After realizing that PJ was again unconscious, the doctor began to again place his medical needle in and out of PJ's body. Another terrible Frankenstein monster sewing job. The killer continued to remain unconscious as the doctor chose to close his wounds and move further down his body. After slicing into the ligaments of PJ's ankles, PJ. wounds were again sewn close with the doctor's medical needle and thread. Upon completion of Dr Dennis's butchery, he was freed from his handcuffs and shackles and left unconscious and naked on the cold metal table. Unbeknownst to PJ the entire butchery was being filmed by several cameras installed in the so-called operation room. Dr Dennis before his departure made sure that the cameras were still operating better yet recording. The quack then said his goodbyes after a long hot shower and headed back to the airport enroute to America. Just after the departure of Dr Dennis the cops also left the area, that is all except the lone officer who had been assigned to monitor the serial killer overnight.

The policeman and an accomplice placed the unconscious man on a stretcher and wheeled him back upstairs before placing him back into his cage.

Photo courtesy of Shannon G.

CHAPTER NINE
THE RECOVERY

Okay Mr. PJ said the officer to the unconscious killer. We're back... We're back to the recovery room. If you need anything, anything at all, just give me a buzz. Stated the cop after letting out a demonic snicker. The tortured PJ was placed on his bunk by the men who then exited the cage and place both padlocks on the cage door'

PJ never regained consciousness that night nor did he the next day, this worried Billy, the so-called trustee. If PJ died within the next 24 hours then he would lose the bet he placed against the policemen. But the next night PJ regained consciousness and cried out from excruciating pain. He yelled out continually until the trustee graced his presence. As ordered, the trustee entered the cell and administered pain meds to the unfortunate PJ. Within a 20-minute window PJ was again asleep, this time the sleep was medically induced. For some strange reason the thugs were trying to keep PJ comfortable and alive. But this didn't make any sense after all that Dr Dennis had done. It seemed as though the corrupt citizens were slowly trying to murder the killer. For nearly a month PJ was bedridden and unable to move. Anytime he felt the pain was unbearable he was fed a handful of pain meds. After what seems a long period of time, the pain would begin to subside which was a plus to the fugitive/serial killer.

Feeling sure that PJ was out of the woods as far as dying and doing a lot better, his personal trustee decided on giving PJ a mirror. The trustee declared he wanted to show him how his beard had grown. This was just a ploy; the mirror was just another tool used in the psychological torture of PJ. The trustee knew that PJ hadn't viewed himself since losing his ears. Still flat on his back due to being told that movement could cause him to become paralyzed. The so-called trustee held the mirror to PJ's traumatized face, it was then that PJ remembered just what the doctor had done.

"A freak, I look like a freak, why didn't you guys just kill me," he said before bursting out into uncontrollable cries of disbelief and horror.

With a smirk, the jailer spoke out, "I did. I really did vote to kill you, but I was overruled. They wanted you to suffer and stay alive. I wanted you dead. I lost a lot of money betting on you," lied the trustee just before leaving PJ's cage and again administering the padlocks. PJ was so heartbroken that he cried himself to sleep.

It would be nearly a week later when Dr Dennis returned to remove the cast from both arms and legs. His wounds seem to have completely healed. But something was amiss PJ thought to himself. He still couldn't move either his legs, or his fingers. His body was completely limp, the only thing the fugitive/serial killer was able to move was his head and mouth. With the trustees help, the doctor placed PJ's feet on the floor, then helped the former gravedigger to his feet. The doctor and trustee looked into each other's eyes, the doctor nodded and both men released PJ to stand by his own footing. But that would remain to be seen. PJ's body fell to the floor like discarded jello. Both men cheered then the doctor spoke out. "You are now totally handicapped Mr. PJ; your killing days are behind you now. You will never be able to walk or feed yourself without the assistance of another. You won't even be able to clean yourself alone. The only thing useful to you are your organs and that useless piehole you call a mouth," stated the butcher of a doctor. After his lecture the doctor gathered his belongings and left the crippled serial killer alone to ponder on the life he would have as a cripple. Later that day PJ was dressed and prepared to be released from his torture chamber. The corrupt individuals had planned to escort PJ and release him in the worst parts of the city. The crippled PJ would be placed in an alley for others to find him. It was a horrible thought that went through the ex-gravedigger's mind. He wasn't able to walk. He couldn't even use his hands to feed himself. There was no way that he could survive alone, let alone on the streets of a city abroad. Streets where he knew no one. But just as the doctor was beginning to gather up the crippled serial killer's belongings the building was surrounded by gunmen. Little did anyone know those gunmen were allowed into the city by government officials and federal law enforcement agents. Most of the gunmen were federal law enforcement from the United States. A few days prior there was a brief internal investigation by the local police department, afterwards the female officer was detained and questioned. After hours of interrogation, the now ex-female officer finally admitted that she knew the whereabouts of the ex-prisoner.

Better yet the location of what the police chief thought was an escaped prisoner. The cooperation of the country's Federal officials and law enforcement agencies along with United States federal agents wasted no time locating the rundown building that housed the wanted fugitive. The corrupt police male officers were all killed in a short gun battle. Doctor Dennis was also captured and placed in police custody. A shell of a man known as PJ was finally rescued by the law enforcement officials. He was unrecognizable, the shell of a man now weighed merely one hundred and ten pounds. Although PJ figured that his life was over, he shed tears of joy seeing the federal agents of the United States. After a few days of negotiations, the sought-after fugitive was released into the custody of United States law enforcement agents. After a short hospital stay the highly sought-after PJ was now aboard a flight enroute back to the good ole USA. Upon his return to the states PJ was admitted into a naval hospital where he received much needed care for the butchery performed by evil Doctor Dennis. After months of receiving several intense surgeries and months upon months of rehabilitation, the battered PJ was again able to use his limbs again.

In the midst of all the reconstructive surgeries and all the much-needed rehabilitation, not once did PJ wish he'd lived a different life. Never did he pray and ask for forgiveness for all the wrongs he'd committed. His only thoughts were how he could escape, join another crime family and of course extract his revenge on the Vonbe family

The ears that had been removed from PJ were replaced. Although his new ears were not of human flesh he again resembled his old self. He often praised the surgeon who performed his cosmetic surgery. After the attachment of his artificial ears and assurance that he was totally healed by the medical procedures, he was released from his doctor's care. PJ was then placed in a federal prison where he would remain until his trial for the murders he'd committed. Not counting the murders he committed abroad, but the number of killings was documented at sixty-seven. Sixty-seven US citizens killed at the hands of PJ Parker. The killer was now known as one of the United States' most infamous serial killers. After years of trials and incarcerations, PJ was sentenced to life without the possibility of parole. This sentence angered many of his victims' loved ones. There were those who wanted and demanded the death sentence. But the sentence was officially life without the possibility of parole for PJ. He was housed in a federal facility for over 10 years after his sentence was handed down. Once he'd served out ten years in federal custody; he was handed over to state prison officials to live out the rest of his sentence in state prison. But PJ wouldn't live past 55 years of age, due to being brutally murdered by his cellmate. His death was all over his repeated cheating during a card game. It was a gruesome scene, PJ's blood crept. along the prison dorm's cement floor, making its way out of PJ's cell and down the dorm's passageway. The killer had finally died as he lived. Many wondered what his last thoughts were as he took his last breath. His last thoughts were " Once I recover from these wounds, I'll have my revenge" That day would never come.

Doctor Dennis was also placed in police custody where he would be held until his trial. It was ironic that the doctor was found guilty of mutilating and murdering a total of sixty-seven people. Dr. Dennis was not so lucky as to live as long as PJ had. He would live just long enough to be tried by his country's legal system, then once found guilty the butcher was sentenced to hang by the neck until death.

Scott was still as cocky as ever and still positive his crime associates would somehow liberate him from police custody. The doctor slept without any worries that night. Even until the trapdoor flung open beneath his feet; Scott Dennis was still sure that the Vonbe crime family would rescue him. Nothing could have been farther from the truth. At that point the Vonbe family felt as though it was time for a younger member of the medical profession to join their criminal organization

The very next morning after his hanging. his body wouldn't be turned over to his family members. The doctor would be loaded into a police SUV, driven into a nearby jungle, and his body discarded. The evil doctor's body would be devoured by the animals of that jungle. Doctor Dennis, like PJ, also died as he'd lived. The world had finally cleansed itself of two of its most ruthless killers, making the world a better, more secure place. Both men undeniably lived reckless lives, but in the end, krama had its say.

THE END

Acknowledgements

I'd like to thank all of those who inspired me to write the story, such as my wife Thearesa L. Stevens and my publisher Tony Anuci. Also, I'd like to give special thanks to my friends (listed below) who donated pictures used in The Graves novelette.

Author E.N.Chanting
Colin Hill
P.J Parker
Sage Marchant
Brandie She Travels For Lunch
Ruthanne Jagge
Cornelius S.
Shannon G.
Thank you all!

Printed in the USA
CPSIA information can be obtained
at www.ICGtesting.com
CBHW072115110724
11457CB00014B/620